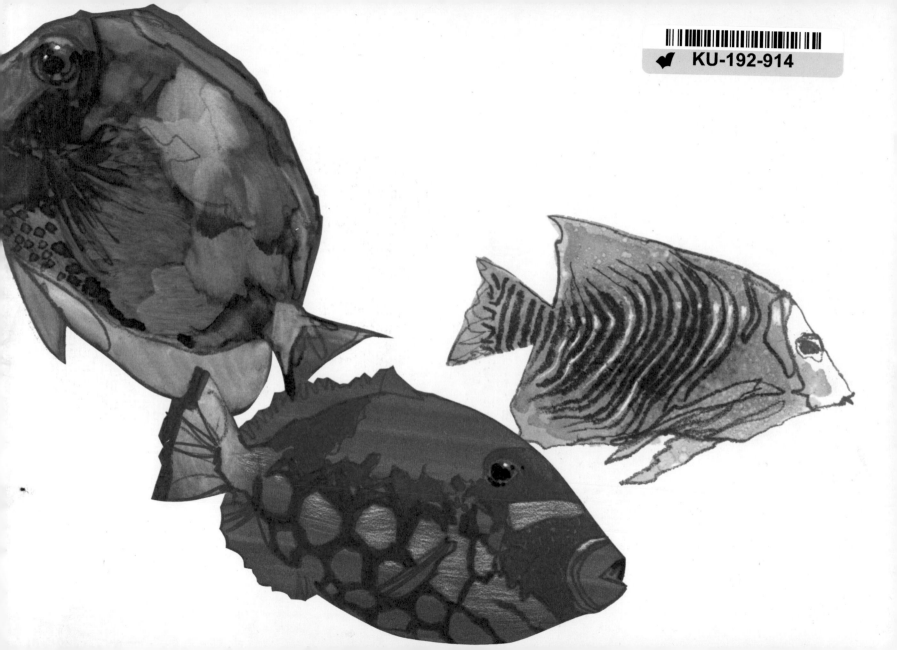

This book has been written
especially for Ewan.

From

If you are lucky enough to meet someone who wants to be your best friend, sooner or later you will want to know where this super friend lives. Well, you won't meet anyone nicer or merrier than Wizwam. But just try asking him where he lives and you will probably get the reply, "Oh, just here–there–everywhere!" And if that doesn't satisfy you and you ask him again, he may tell you that somewhere–at a point where the rainbow ends–he has a cosy little place which he calls home.

Lots of wizards, of course, spend all their lives in just one place with their Spell-books, their black pots and their toads. But Wizwam isn't that kind of wizard at all. He spends all his time just WIZWAMMING around. He's what you might call a 'man-of-action' wizard, which means that he doesn't have much time left over for his rainbow house. And that is just one of the reasons why he always wears his fantastic, dazzling, rainbow cloak; it reminds him of home!

Another reason is that his wonderful cloak has huge deep pockets which come in very useful when he is suddenly called upon to perform some really difficult wizard magic.

Wizwam doesn't pretend to be a very high-class wizard, and just in case his magic doesn't work first time, he takes along Sunny. If you take a close look at Wizwam you can see Sunny, the giant magic sunflower, sitting in his buttonhole.

Now, one of the really super things about Wizwam is that he never goes on a wizwamming adventure all by himself. He takes along a friend to share in the fun. Of course, it has to be a very special little friend, and by special invitation only!

A wizwamming wizard like Wizwam doesn't send out invitations. He just arrives–then the fun begins. And who do you think is going to share Wizwam's Adventure this time? You've guessed it first time. It's lucky YOU!

ISBN 0 905112 02 4 COPYRIGHT © 1975 PERSONAL BOOKS LIMITED
Published by Personal Books Limited, 225 Goldhawk Road, London W12 8ER. All rights reserved.
Printed by Chorley & Pickersgill Ltd Leeds

# Wizwam and Ewan under the Sea

Story by Jane Carruth
Pictures by Cab Richardson

Of all the wizards in the world
there is none so merry, so full of
wizard magic as Wizwam. That was why
it was such a big thrill for Ewan
when Wizwam paid him a surprise visit.

"Do tell me you are Ewan,"
the wizard said after he had quickly
introduced himself. "It's not so easy
finding one's way about these days.
I used to count the smoking chimneys,
but with all this central heating ..."

"Well, you've found ME," Ewan
interrupted, his eyes sparkling.

"That is a relief," Wizwam smiled.
"To begin with I wasn't even sure of
finding Munlochy."

"I know we're going to have some kind of an adventure," Ewan burst out.

"You're right," replied the wizard. "We are going to pay my old friend, the Sea King, a visit. He has a nice little place on the coral reef. What do you say?"

"I'd love it!" Ewan gasped. "How do we get there?"

"Ah, well, you leave that to me," said Wizwam. "But you could help by repeating WIZWAM after me, if you like."

"Wizwam – wizwam!" he repeated obediently.

They landed with a bump on the sea-bed, and Wizwam pushed up the hatch of his super two-man flying sea-saucer.

"We've arrived!" he announced.

Goodness – it was beautiful under the sea! There were pink trees of twisting coral, and bright darting fishes, some splashed with blue, red and orange. The gay sea-flowers and tall waving sea grasses were so pretty that it was hard to believe they were really growing deep down under the sea.

"It's just like a wonderful fairy-land garden!" Ewan exclaimed.

"How I'd love to show all this to Martin."

"I thought you would like it," said Wizwam, looking pleased. "The Sea King's palace is behind that big rock . . ." He broke off as, out of the shadows, a huge, ugly fish came gliding towards him.

"Look out!" Ewan shouted.

But Wizwam knew how to deal with the monster. No sooner had he touched his giant sunflower than a beam of light shot out, dazzling the attacking fish. Bewildered, it stopped in its tracks, then swam off in disgust.

The Sea King's palace stood in a charming garden of sea-flowers. The King himself was seated on a throne of shells under a canopy of red coral. Wizwam gave him a cheerful greeting, explaining that he had brought a very special young friend to see him.

"This is my friend, Ewan," he said finally. "He has come all the way from Ross and Cromarty."

As the King nodded to Ewan, Wizwam whispered, "Don't stare at his feet – I mean royal tail. You will soon get used to it."

"What is he holding in his hand?" Ewan whispered back.

"That is his trident," the wizard told him. "Neptune gave it to him."

To their surprise, the King suddenly blew his nose. Then two salty tears, as big as pearls, rolled down his cheeks into his white beard.

"Hide behind that pillar," Wizwam ordered. "I must have a private talk with His Majesty."

"I've never seen a King cry before – I wonder what can be wrong?" Ewan asked himself, as he crouched behind one of the coral pillars. "It must be serious to make a King cry."

After Wizwam had talked with the King for a while, His Majesty clapped his hands and five very pretty mermaids, all exactly alike, came out from behind some of the pillars. They wore crowns of coral and anemones on their heads and their golden hair was so long that it fell over their shoulders.

They formed a line in front of the throne, and first the King and then Wizwam solemnly counted them.

"One – two – three – four – five . . ." Wizwam counted. And he shook his head. Then he counted the Princesses all over again, and the answer was still the same. There were only five and there should be six. No wonder the King was unhappy!

"I've promised His Majesty that we will search for the missing Princess," Wizwam began as he joined Ewan. "The King is sure the parrot fish have taken her prisoner, but we'll soon find out."

As he spoke they entered a dark, gloomy forest. "This is Seaweed Forest," he continued, "and over there . . . ."

". . . are the parrot fish!" Ewan shouted. "Just look at their horrid beaky mouths!"

"You're right," Wizwam agreed, "and that black hole between the rocks must be the entrance to their grotto. They could be holding the Princess there out of revenge. It seems the old King lost his temper when they started nibbling his coral pillars."

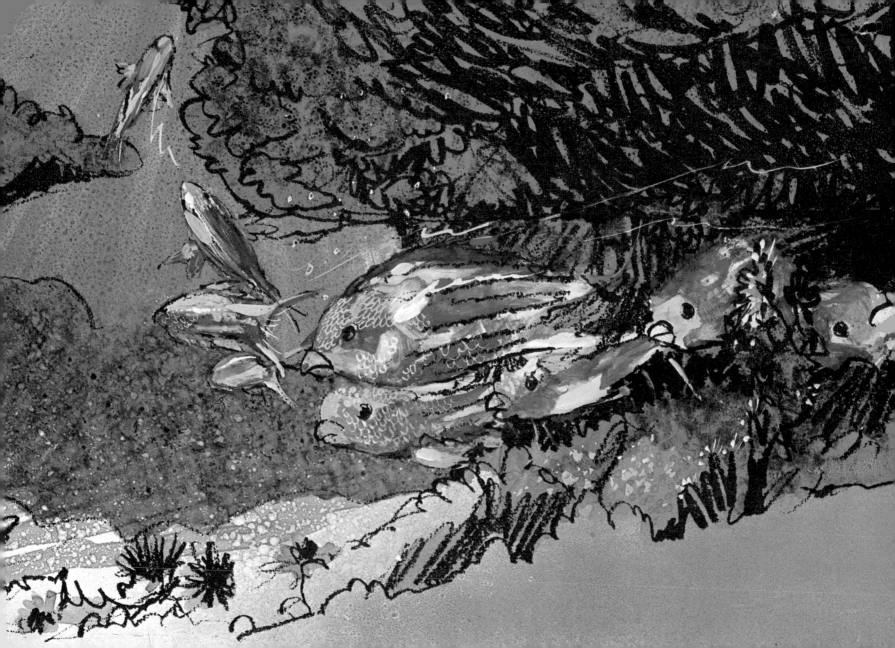

Then, greatly daring, Wizwam rushed after the red and yellow fish.

"Hi! Wait for me!" cried Ewan. And, screwing up all his courage, he went after the wizard.

Once inside the grotto, he rubbed his eyes in astonishment. It was filled with the most fantastic monsters which, in the pale green light, looked terrifyingly real.

"Don't worry," Wizwam called. "They're not real – they're made of coral."

"I don't believe the Princess is here after all," Ewan decided, watching the fish as they nibbled the coral with their strong beaky mouths. "I must tell Wizwam . . ."

When he looked up, Wizwam had vanished.

"You can't scare me!" Ewan shouted at the coral monsters towering above him. But he would have given anything to have had his collie, Jill for company.

As suddenly as he had vanished Wizwam re-appeared – riding on the back of a giant sea turtle.

"This way!" Ewan shouted, and he held up his hand as if he were about to stop a bus in faraway Ross and Cromarty.

"Jump on behind," Wizwam ordered. And, breathless with excitement, Ewan obeyed.

What a story he would have to tell Lorna.

"Hold tight!" Wizwam shouted over his shoulder, as the turtle sped through the water. "I think I know where we shall find the missing Princess."

"Where are we going?" Ewan managed to gasp out.

For answer, Wizwam pointed ahead. "There she is." he exclaimed. "A mighty ghost ship of the past! Whoa, turtle! We've arrived."

As they slid off the turtle's broad back, Wizwam said, "That wreck was once a famous pirate ship. Now she belongs to the sea..."

"And to the fishes," added Ewan, his eyes dancing.

The skeleton of the great ship looked dark and forbidding as they clambered aboard. But, as they began to explore, they were followed everywhere by shoals of little fishes as brightly coloured as tropical butterflies.

With the help of Sunny's strong clear light they came upon the little mermaid at last. There she sat – in the shadow of the ship's lantern – and there, beside her, was the pirates' very own treasure chest, brimming over with gold.

"Just as I guessed," said Wizwam. "She ran away to play with all this glittering treasure. This must be her secret playground."

"I'm so glad we found her," whispered Ewan.

"Now we must take her back to the palace," Wizwam went on.

"And the treasure?"

"No," replied the wizard. "We'll leave it all here where it belongs."

The old Sea King was so happy to have his youngest daughter safely home again that he forgot to scold her for running away.

He stroked his long, white beard, and two tears, as big as pearls, ran down his cheeks. But the wizard knew they were tears of joy.

Then he made a speech inviting Wizwam and his brave friend to a great feast in their honour. And some of the pretty girl-fishes hung a garland of flowers around the wizard's neck, which made him smile broadly.

The feast was soon prepared. It was the most wonderful banquet imaginable, and lasted for hours.

After such a splendid feast, it was no
wonder everybody began to look very sleepy.
"Don't sleep now," Wizwam warned his young
friend. "It is time to go home."

The Sea King and his six lovely daughters came
with them to their super flying sea-saucer.
"I will never, never forget you all,"
promised Ewan.

"And we will never, never forget YOU,"
chorused the lovely Princesses. Then
Wizwam pulled him aboard their craft, and
closed the hatch.

"I wish I had asked the runaway mermaid her
name – I meant to," Ewan murmured sleepily.
And, as the saucer lifted off the sea-bed,
he covered his mouth with his hand to hide a
monster-sized yawn.

"Now is the time for a long, happy sleep,"
Wizwam whispered softly. "Goodbye, my friend. Your
Wizwam Adventure is over – until the next time!"

THE END